Animal Antics

THE CLUMSY MONKEY

For Bertie, who has monkeys where he lives – LC

For Emily – PA

STRIPES PUBLISHING
An imprint of Magi Publications
1 The Coda Centre, 189 Munster Road,
London SW6 6AW

A paperback original
First published in Great Britain in 2011

Text copyright © Lucy Courtenay, 2011
Illustrations copyright © Phil Alderson, 2011

ISBN: 978-1-84715-166-7

The right of Lucy Courtenay and Phil Alderson to
be identified as the author and illustrator of this work
respectively has been asserted by them in accordance
with the Copyright, Designs and Patents Act, 1988.

Printed and bound in the UK.

10 9 8 7 6 5 4 3 2 1

Animal Antics

THE CLUMSY MONKEY

LUCY COURTENAY

Illustrated by Phil Alderson

Stripes

Animals!

Everyone loves animals. Feathery, furry, fierce. Scaly, scary, hairy. Cute, a bit smelly, all-round bonkers.

But let's be honest. How well do we really know them?
I know my dog, you might say.
I know my cat and my hamster.

Ah, I say. You may think you know them, but you DON'T.
When you watch them, they do catty
and doggy and hamstery things.
But what about when you're not watching?
Who knows what they do when you're snoozing
in your beds or when you're at school?

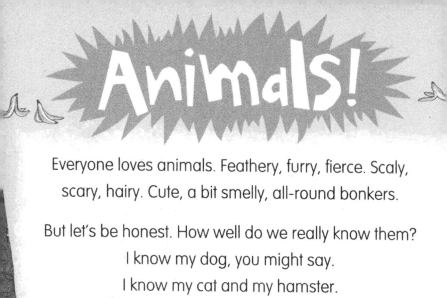

And what about the rest of the animal kingdom?
The world is full of amazing creatures –
from camels in the desert, to baboons
in the forest, and fish in the deepest ocean.

We know even less about them.
For all we know, they might like dancing. Or doing
handstands. Or playing thumb wars. Actually, not that
one because most animals don't have thumbs.
But you know what I mean.

Maybe we don't know animals as well as we think.
Take **MONKEYS,** for instance…

Chapter One

It was a hot and steamy dawn in the rainforest. The topmost branches of the highest trees were lost in the mist. So were the middle branches. In fact, the whole jungle was misty from top to bottom.

"Wake up, you lazybones troop!" came a commanding voice. "There's food to eat and fur to groom and lots of stuff to do today!"

Monkeys began to stir in the branches. Down near the ground there was a flop and a crash.

"OUCH!"

Morris the monkey had just fallen off his night perch, knocking several bugs to the ground. They scuttled off, complaining in squeaky voices.

HEY!

Animal Antics

"Well, really!"

"Can't an insect get a bit of peace?"

Morris rubbed his furry brown head. "Sorry," he said awkwardly.

He was always falling off branches and disturbing bugs. Even when the jungle mist wasn't making it difficult to see, Morris fell out of trees. He also walked *into* trees and punched other monkeys in his troop by accident.

"Is that you, Morris?" came the commanding voice again. "Are you all right?"

Morris peered upwards. "I'm fine, Mum," he said. "OUCH," he added, as he scraped the top of his head on a twig.

"Of course it's Morris," said another voice, higher up in the mist. "Who else says 'ouch' fifty times a day?"

"Marvin, don't be rude to your brother," said Morris's mum.

Animal Antics

"I don't do it on purpose, Marvin," said Morris. "OUCH!" he added again, as he stubbed his toe on a gnarled tree root that was poking up through the leaf litter.

Morris's big brother Marvin swung down through the branches and landed lightly on his feet beside him. Marvin didn't bump into anything. Marvin never knocked things over. And if he punched the other monkeys in the troop, it was usually part of some stupid joke he was playing. In short, Morris and Marvin were complete opposites.

"Do you need some help to get back up the tree, Morris?" said Marvin with a smirk.

"No, thanks," Morris said. He knew what his brother meant by "help". He meant he'd hold Morris's paw just long enough to get him off the ground – and then drop him on his head for a laugh. "I'm fine."

Animal Antics

"Well, if you're sure…" Marvin said.

Morris waved one paw casually, knocking his elbow on the tree trunk. "I'm sure," he said, trying his best not to say "ouch" again.

"Fine," said Marvin, shooting off. "See you!" Morris heard him moving up the misty tree like lightning. Jump, bound, jump and leap. Morris knew that Marvin would be back in the jungle canopy within minutes.

The troop screeched and whooped overhead, making their usual racket. Morris sighed and glanced around the jungle floor. Perhaps he could live on the ground for a bit and skip the whole tree-jumping thing. There was plenty of food. But rhesus macaque monkeys like Morris didn't live on the ground. There were too many leopards and pythons and other predators, waiting to… Well, it was just safer in the trees.

But safer for whom? Morris wondered. Not for him, because he was always falling out of them. And not for the monkeys he knocked off the branches whenever he was passing.

Animal Antics

You're a rhesus macaque monkey, Morris told himself. *Rhesus macaques live in trees. It's in your blood. You can do it. Just JUMP!*

Jump, bound … *bump.*

"OUCH."

Bound, leap … *crash.*

"OOF!"

Jump, swing, leaaaaaaaaaa—

"OW!" howled an unfortunate lizard on the forest floor as Morris fell on top of it.

"He's a menace, that Morris," said a stripey bug nearby, as the lizard limped away.

"He shouldn't live in the trees," agreed a spotty bug.

"Maybe he's not a monkey at all," suggested a plain bug.

Animal Antics

"Do you mind not talking about me like I'm not here?" said Morris, getting to his feet.

"His family must be so ashamed," said the stripey bug.

"I would be," said the spotty one.

"Whoever heard of a clumsy monkey?" said the plain one.

Morris had never considered this before. But now he came to think of it, they were probably right. After all, his mother was the boss of the troop, and his brother was brilliant at climbing and swinging.

Animal Antics

I'm an embarrassment, Morris thought in horror. *That's what I am. An embarrassment!*

Suddenly, Morris heard soft thumps and loud voices all around him in the white, swirling mist. His troop had come down the tree in search of food.

"Hello, Morris," said his mum, rumpling the fur on his head affectionately. "Ooh, papaya!" she added, and reached over to a pile of yellow fruit. "I knew it was worth coming down! Early morning is always the best time of day to feed on the ground. Didn't I tell you, everyone?"

The troop nodded, their cheeks bulging with fruit and juice running down their furry chins. Morris's troop were only ever quiet when they were eating.

"You're the boss, Mum," said Marvin.

"Don't be a creep, Marvin," she replied. "And don't spit out your pips."

Animal Antics

The other monkeys finished their food and frisked around, laughing and shouting. Morris stayed very still, trying hard not to tread on anyone's toes and listening to the silly jokes everyone was telling.

"Hey, Matthew!" called Marvin. "Did you hear the one about the monkey who went bananas?"

"Ha ha! Good one, Marvin! What's white and fluffy and beats its chest?"

"Uh…"

Morris leaped into the air. He knew the answer!

"OW!" yelled Marvin, clapping his paws over his face as Morris whacked him in the nose. "You clumsy oaf!"

Morris was about to apologize when there was a faint rustling in the misty undergrowth. Was it a leopard? A python?

Animal Antics

"Quick!" Morris's mum ordered. "Everyone up the tree!"

In two seconds flat, the only monkey left on the jungle floor was Morris.

"A *meringue*-utan," said Morris sadly, as his mum leaned down and yanked him to safety.

Chapter Two

"I've had a brilliant idea, Morris," said his mother the next morning.

Morris felt a sense of doom. His mother was always thinking of crazy ways to cure his clumsiness. They never worked.

"Gymnastics classes!" said his mother.

"What?" said Morris in disbelief.

"Gymnastics classes," his mum repeated.

Animal Antics

"Magda teaches the youngsters most days."

She nodded across to the big kapok tree opposite. Drifting on the wind, Morris heard old Magda's booming voice shouting instructions.

"Left and SWING and right and SWING and OVER the branch we go. Good work, Molly! Nice try, Mac! Bad luck, Minty, dear!"

Morris was horrorstruck. Apart from anything else, gymnastics classes were for the youngest monkeys in the troop. He'd been to Magda's classes himself as soon as he had stopped hanging off his mother's belly. They hadn't been a success. He couldn't go back and do more classes with all those babies. He just *couldn't*. He glanced around nervously for his brother. Marvin would find the idea hilarious.

"I'm sure Magda's class is the answer to your little problem," Morris's mum went on. "I've already spoken to her and she's expecting you this afternoon."

Morris wrapped his arms round the tree trunk. He was feeling a little dizzy.

"Can't I just—" he began.

"*No*, Morris." His mum wasn't the most important monkey in the troop for nothing. "You're going this afternoon," she repeated, in a steely sort of voice.

That afternoon, Morris sat miserably in the branches in front of Magda. There were twenty other monkeys in the class, and they were all half Morris's size. Nearly everyone looked excited. The noise was deafening. Several youngsters were already practising leaps, bounds and jumps among the branches. Morris wrapped his tail extra tightly round the branch he was sitting on.

Animal Antics

Marvin sat in the tree opposite, watching gleefully. "We're not going to fall out of the tree *too* often today, are we, Morris?" he shouted, in a perfect imitation of Magda's booming voice.

"That's quite enough from you, Marvin!" boomed Magda.

I will, Morris thought. *I know I will.*

"First of all," said Magda, "grip your branch with those tails!"

All the monkeys gripped on to the branches with their tails. Morris gripped extra *extra* tightly.

"Now drop backwards and swing round in a full circle!"

Most of the class swung round their branches at once. Morris and two of the littlest monkeys stared at Magda with scared eyes and didn't move.

Magda gave the first monkey a brisk shove.

Animal Antics

Clinging on with his tail, he swung backwards round the branch in a neat circle with a look of surprise on his small pink face. The second youngster got the same treatment.

"Your turn, Morris," Magda said, in a voice that made Morris urgently need the loo.

Her paw shot out and shoved him hard in the chest. Because Morris was much heavier than the other two, he whizzed round one … two … three times, coming to a perfect stop back on top of the branch again.

"You see?" said Magda. "Not difficult at all."

Morris grinned. *Maybe I'm not such an embarrassment after all*, he thought.

"Let's try that again, shall we?" said Magda. "And … swing!"

Obediently, Morris fell backwards off his branch and let his tail swing him round. On his third go, he tried to beat his three-spin record.

Animal Antics

He managed four and a half.

I'm not bad at this! Morris felt pleased as he pulled himself back up again. Suddenly, he was glad that his mother had made him come to Magda's classes.

"Last time!" Magda called.

Morris hurled himself backwards so fast that he whizzed round his branch five times – and lost his grip.

"Help!" Morris shouted. With his paws scrabbling at nothing, he rocketed into the air and crashed hard into the upper branches. The tree shuddered. Fluffy kapok seeds fell like tiny clouds to the ground. And, along with at least a thousand bugs, the entire class fell out of the tree.

"Waaah!" wailed the little monkeys as they plummeted towards the jungle floor at great speed.

Animal Antics

"WAAAH!" they wailed even louder, as they hit the ground with a tremendous thump.

Everyone – except for Marvin, who was laughing too hard – poured out of the treetops and rushed to help the youngsters.

"Oh my coconuts!" gasped Morris's mum.

"Molly!"

"Mummyyyyyyyy!"

There were just two monkeys left in the kapok tree. Magda was gazing down at the heap of bent tails, bruised paws and bumped heads on the jungle floor. Higher up the tree, Morris was wedged upside down between two forked branches. The sound of twenty howling youngsters, fifty worried adults and a thousand furious beetles filled the air.

Morris opened his mouth to say sorry.

"Not a word, Morris," Magda said. "Not. One. Word."

Chapter Three

That evening, Morris hunched all alone on a low branch in the kapok tree. The rest of the troop were settling down for the night higher up the tree, shouting and yelling the way they always did. He could hear Marvin joking with his friends.

"Hey, what do you call a monkey with no brain?"

Animal Antics

"Morris!"

"Why did the monkey fall out of the tree?"

"Because his name was Morris!"

"What do you get if you cross a monkey with an elephant?"

"Morris!"

His mum had been very nice about the kapok tree thing, but Morris felt sure she was embarrassed deep down. And now his brother was making sure the whole troop was laughing at him.

He hunched closer to the tree trunk. Night was coming, and the darkness was squeezing around the trees like a huge and hungry python. He knew he should climb to a higher branch, but he couldn't face seeing anyone just now.

He jumped at the sound of small voices. It was the three bugs from the day before.

"Still here, are you?" said the stripey bug.

"Thought you'd have left by now," said the spotty one.

"Your troop doesn't want you any more," said the plain one.

There was a scream of laughter overhead.

"They're laughing at you," said the plain bug.

"You should go," said the spotty one.

"Make like a tree and leave," said the stripey one. "Get it? Leave? *Leaf?*"

The young monkey had never felt so bad in his life. He knew the bugs were right. His mother only let him stay in the troop out of pity. Marvin would be glad to see him go.

Yes, Morris thought. *It is time to leave.*

He looked out at the darkness. Then before he could change his mind, he jumped off his branch, stumbled and began to run.

Morris ran, fell over and ran some more. He was too terrified to stop, so he kept going. There were strange noises in the jungle at night. Rustling and hooting. Scratching and purring. Echoing and crackling. Morris speeded up. Soon he was covered in leaves and scratches from head to foot.

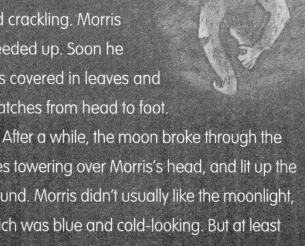

After a while, the moon broke through the trees towering over Morris's head, and lit up the ground. Morris didn't usually like the moonlight, which was blue and cold-looking. But at least he could see where he was going now.

Panting and frightened, he looked around. He didn't know this part of the jungle. But where

Animal Antics

there was jungle, there were trees.

I need to get off the ground, he thought.

Too many things with hungry tummies prowled the jungle by night. Too many things that liked snacking on monkeys.

He chose a tree with an extra wide trunk. A strangler fig vine dangled down. Morris grabbed the vine and hauled himself off the ground. Puffing and blowing like a forest rhinoceros, Morris climbed as high as he dared. Then he crouched on a branch and shut his eyes, hoping to catch some sleep before something hungry caught *him*.

The jungle is never silent. But without the grunts and snores of his troop in the branches above, Morris's tree felt like the quietest tree in the world. It was so quiet that he couldn't sleep.

Animal Antics

I'll try counting bugs, Morris decided.

But all he could think about were the ones who'd been so mean to him, which didn't help him get to sleep at all. He lay flat on the branch, then panicked as he felt himself sliding off sideways. As he tried to get comfortable, Morris thought of his mum. Had she noticed he'd gone?

"She'll be glad," he said sadly to himself. "I only embarrassed her."

He shut his eyes tightly and waited. But still sleep didn't come.

Animal Antics

With a sigh, Morris opened his eyes again. It was no good. He needed to find a noisier tree. One with monkeys in it.

He took hold of the strangler fig vine and scrambled down to the jungle floor.

"Ooh!" said a large furry someone as Morris landed on its back.

Morris leaped in fright. It was too dark to see what he'd landed on. With a squeal of terror, he scrabbled to get off the creature's back, tripped and cartwheeled through the air.

A flash of moonlight illuminated the ground. To Morris's horror, he was falling towards a Thing. A dark, round Thing. A Thing that looked like a wide-open mouth.

Chapter Four

Morris pedalled his arms and legs frantically.
He swung his tail from left to right hopelessly.
And he landed smack in the middle of the Thing.

"OOOF!"

Morris wriggled. His head and shoulders
were stuck fast. With a mixture of dismay and
relief, he realized that he'd landed head-first in
an extremely smelly hole in the ground.

Animal Antics

Morris heard a muffled shout somewhere behind him.

"Get out of my hole!"

"I can't!" shouted poor Morris, trying not to breathe too much. "I'm stuck!"

He felt a pair of strong paws digging around him.

"Daft monkey," muttered the voice attached to the paws. *Dig, dig, dig.* "Flying about like a bat!" *Dig, dig, dig.* "Monkeys sleep at night! Monkeys don't fall on harmless hog badgers and terrify the wits out of them! Monkeys don't wedge themselves in hog badger holes!"

After a few moments, Morris felt the earth loosen round his shoulders. He dug his back paws into the ground and heaved. With a pop, he flew out of the hog badger's hole and landed on his back.

Animal Antics

A stripey face glared down at him, its pink snout quivering.

"Daft monkey," growled the hog badger again.

Morris got back on to his feet and dusted himself down, pleased to be back in the fresh air. "I'm sorry for all the trouble," he said. "Hope I didn't ruin your hole."

He stuck out a paw in thanks and clonked the hog badger on the chin.

"OW!" roared the hog badger.

Animal Antics

"Oh dear," said Morris hurriedly. "I think I'd better be on my way."

"Brainless nitwit! Twerp with a tail! FURRY GREAT FROG-EATER!"

Morris rushed away from the bellowing hog badger with the insults ringing in his ears.

"Why am I so accident-prone?" he muttered to himself in despair.

He hurried along a moonlit track, glancing left and right. He listened for familiar monkey noises among the dark trees overhead, hoping to find a troop that might let him live on the lower branches of their tree.

The darkness is so confusing! thought poor Morris. *Where am I?*

His heart thumping, Morris darted among the shadows and scampered between the tree trunks, expecting something to close its jaws round him with a SNAP. And just as he was thinking how he hadn't bumped into anything for a while, he crashed into the back end of a porcupine.

"OW!" Morris yelled, hopping about in agony. As he pulled the quills out of his chest, the porcupine shuffled round to look at him in the moonlight.

"What's the rush?" she said.

Morris yanked out the last quill and gave his chest a rub. "I don't want to be eaten!" he said. "It's a good reason for hurrying!"

"Nothing will eat you while you're with me," said the porcupine.

Morris stopped rubbing his chest. "Oh really? Why not?"

The porcupine rustled her quills at him. Morris understood at once. He imagined very few creatures ever wanted to attack a porcupine on purpose.

"What's a young monkey like you doing out on a night like this?" asked the porcupine.

The porcupine sounded like his mother, only a bit quieter. It made Morris feel so terribly homesick that he burst into tears. The porcupine stood beside him, licking the tears from his face.

"Th-th-thanks," Morris snuffled. "Sorry to be so silly."

"Don't thank me," said the porcupine. "Thank *you*. I needed those tears. I haven't had a good salt lick in days."

Morris blinked. "Oh," he said. "That's OK."

"I hope my quills didn't hurt too much," the porcupine said.

Morris's chest was still stinging where the quills had stabbed him. "I hardly felt them," he lied. "It was my fault for not looking where I was going."

"Where *are* you going?" the porcupine asked.

Morris was so grateful for the porcupine's kindness and interest that he sat down in the middle of the jungle floor and began to tell his story. The porcupine listened, munching every now and again on a piece of tree bark.

"So you've left home for good?" she said, when Morris finished telling her about the accident in Magda's class and the rude bugs, his horrible brother and the nasty hog badger.

"Looks like it," he said gloomily. "I'm just an embarrassment. Especially to my mother. She's the boss of the troop, you see."

"You can stay with me for a while if you like," said the porcupine. "And if you could cry every few days," she added, "that would be perfect."

"Thanks," said Morris. He glanced around the jungle floor. "But to be honest, I don't feel very safe on the ground. Even with you beside me. So I'd better get going."

"Shame," said the porcupine, looking disappointed. "Well, good luck. And watch out for leopards. They've been prowling around these parts."

Morris swallowed nervously at the mention of leopards. Finding a tree with monkeys in it felt more important than ever.

"Bye then," he said.

"Goodbye," said the porcupine. "And next time you feel like crying, come and find me again, will you?"

Chapter Five

The jungle was beautiful at night. There were strange flowers Morris had never seen before, filling the air with sweet smells. There were little animals with wide-open eyes, hanging in the trees, who looked even more scared of him than he was of them. Moonshadows made lovely patterns on the leafy jungle floor.

Animal Antics

If I weren't so tired and frightened of being eaten, Morris thought, *I might start enjoying this little adventure.*

Suddenly, his foot landed on something cold and scaly. He lifted it away at once, feeling scared. Snakes were cold and scaly. Snakes – big ones, at least – ate monkeys.

The cold scaly thing twitched. With a sigh of relief, Morris realized that it was someone's tail. "Sorry," he said quickly.

"Sorry for what?" said the someone, turning its head and blinking at him.

"For treading on your tail," said Morris, his eyes widening.

He was looking at the weirdest creature he'd ever seen. It was covered in brown scales from head to toe. It had a long snout and tiny ears. As Morris watched, it shot out a very long tongue and scooped up a mouthful of ants.

Animal Antics

"Did you tread on my tail?" said the creature, chewing. "I didn't notice."

"Oh," said Morris, surprised. "You really didn't feel it?"

"Pangolins never feel things like having their tails trodden on," said the creature. It nodded at its scales.

"Do your scales protect you?" Morris asked.

The pangolin nodded again.

Animal Antics

Morris could hardly believe his ears. At last, someone he couldn't hurt! He gave a little jump of joy.

"Sorry!" he said, as he landed on the pangolin's foot.

"Sorry for what?" said the pangolin again.

Morris wanted to cheer. He wanted to jump again. And maybe he'd land on the pangolin's tail AND its foot this time, and it STILL wouldn't shout at him.

"Do you like ants?" asked the pangolin.

"I love ants!" said Morris in delight. "My name is Morris, by the way."

"Hello, Morris," said the pangolin. "I'm Pan."

Morris sat with Pan for a while and ate a few ants.

"What else do you like doing?" said Morris, when they'd eaten. "Apart from eating ants?"

"I like climbing trees," said Pan.

Animal Antics

Morris's heart sank. "I'm not very good at climbing trees."

Now it was Pan's turn to look surprised. "But I thought monkeys spent all day in the trees," he said.

"Not me," said Morris glumly. "I spend all day falling OUT of trees. I've left home because I'm an embarrassment. And I keep hurting everyone because I'm so clumsy."

"You haven't hurt me," Pan pointed out.

"I know," said Morris, feeling happier again. "Fantastic, isn't it?"

Pan suddenly sniffed the air. "I think," he said, "I can smell leopards."

Morris's tummy lurched. "Leopards eat monkeys! Do they eat pangolins?"

"Oh yes," said Pan.

"Then we have to get out of here!" said Morris, jumping to his feet.

Animal Antics

As they ran towards the nearest tree, there was a crashing sound behind them. It was much too loud to be leopards.

A huge elephant thundered through the moonlit clearing. It snorted loudly as it lifted its tail and shot a heavy ball of dung out of its bottom.

Morris forgot about the leopards. "We need to get off the ground before that elephant

squashes us flat!" he cried.

Pan had stopped running and curled himself into a little armoured ball instead, tucking his nose tightly under his tail. As Morris hurried to get out of the elephant's way, his foot struck the pangolin like a football. Pan went flying through the air, crashed through several branches, ripped a hole in a large leaf and completely disappeared into the night.

Animal Antics

Morris gasped with horror. He scampered as fast as he could towards the place where he had kicked the curled-up pangolin. "Are you OK? Are you there, Pan? I'm sorry! I'm really, really sorry!"

Morris searched until the sun began to peep through the canopy and scatter yellow spots of light on the jungle floor. But no matter how hard he looked, there was no sign of Pan the pangolin.

Not caring if a whole bunch of hungry leopards now turned up and ate him, Morris curled up in a sorry huddle at the base of a big palm tree and hid his face in his paws.

I hope someone comes along soon and eats me and puts me out of my misery, he thought. *Not only am I an embarrassment, but I'm a danger to everyone I meet. At least if I'm someone's lunch, the worst thing that can happen is a nasty bout of indigestion.*

Morris stayed there until the sun began to warm his fur and squeeze between his fingers and stroke his eyelids. Until there was a mighty CRASH … and the palm tree he was hiding under keeled over.

Chapter Six

Morris rocketed into a tree in fright. He saw a bear standing on its hind legs in the misty dawn light. It had an apricot-coloured mark on its black chest that curved upwards like a smile, a black head and an apricot-coloured face.

"Sorry about that," said the bear. "Don't know my own strength."

Morris was trying to remember what he

knew about this sort of bear. "Do you … eat monkeys?" he asked.

The bear blinked. "Sun bears prefer honey, to be honest," he said. "Honey doesn't move as fast as monkeys."

"You're a sun bear?" said Morris.

The bear pointed at the apricot mark on its chest. "Apricot chest equals sun bear," he said. "The name's Sammy. Pleased to meet you."

Sammy waved his paw to say hello and hit himself accidentally on the chin. Then he staggered around and bumped into nearly every tree in the clearing, including the one Morris was sitting in. A rainbow of bugs and brightly coloured frogs cascaded to the jungle floor, alongside Morris.

"Sorry!" said Sammy again. He waved at the bugs and the frogs and whacked an overhanging branch. Three more screeching beetles fell to the ground, plus a coral-coloured snake that hissed angrily before it slithered away.

The sun bear blinked down at Morris. "Here, let me help you up."

Morris ducked, narrowly missing the bear's heavy black paw as it came swinging towards his head.

"Sorry!" said Sammy, yet again.

Morris giggled. Then he clapped his paws over his mouth, feeling bad. He hated it when others laughed at *him*.

"Laugh away," Sammy said cheerfully. "Life in this jungle is one big joke for a sun bear as clumsy as me."

"Really?" said Morris. "You don't mind?"

"Why should I mind?" said Sammy. "I laugh at myself most days. Do you like bananas?"

Morris's tummy rumbled. He hadn't eaten

anything since the ants. He nodded. Sammy
reached out a paw and gave a nearby
banana tree a shove. A heap of bright yellow
fruit showered to the ground.

"Help yourself," Sammy said, sitting down
on a nearby log. "After pushing over your tree,
it's the least I can do."

Morris was starving. He wolfed down so
many bananas, he felt like he was going to pop.

"Aren't you having any?" he said, through a
big mouthful.

Animal Antics

Sammy scratched his bottom and fell off the log he was sitting on. A swarm of ants on the ground rushed off in fright. "You looked hungry," Sammy said, lying on the ground with his stubby black legs in the air. "I can wait. Hey, can we be friends?"

Morris had never made friends with anything clumsier than him before. "Of course we can," he said happily. "I'm Morris, and I'm really, really pleased to meet you, Sammy."

Sammy and Morris spent the morning eating bananas and telling each other their clumsiest stories.

"There was one time," Sammy said, "when I pushed over all the coconut trees on a coconut farm. I didn't mean to. I just pushed over one tree, trying to reach a coconut.

And it fell into the next tree, which fell into the next tree, which fell into the NEXT tree. Soon, there wasn't a single tree left standing. The farmer wasn't very happy about it. Luckily, he was scared of bears."

"I landed head-first in a hog badger's hole last night," said Morris.

"Bet it ponged," said Sammy.

"It did," Morris agreed.

"Have another banana," said Sammy. He reached up and yanked hard on a banana dangling over their heads. The whole bunch crashed down on top of them, followed by the stem that the bunch had been hanging on. Soon, Morris and Sammy were buried in a heap of shiny banana leaves.

Laughing, Morris reached out a paw to move the stem off their heads – and smelled the unmistakable smell of leopards.

Chapter seven

Morris froze. Beside him, Sammy froze too. They peeped through the leaves, hardly daring to breathe.

Two leopards stood in the misty clearing.

"What a useless night," said the bigger leopard crossly. "One measly hog badger and two frogs between us. This is supposed to be the *jungle*. There's *loads* of food in the jungle.

But did we find any? Did we?"

"We found a hog badger and two frogs, Lee," said the second leopard, twitching its tail.

"That's what I just *said*, Laz," said the first leopard. "We need more than that. We're leopards, not lorikeets."

"Lorry what?"

"Keets."

Laz looked confused.

"Birds, Laz – birds," Lee said impatiently.

Laz gazed around with interest. "Where?"

Lee rolled his eyes.

Morris sat as still as he could. He was hot and uncomfortable. The banana stem was almost squashing him flat.

"We need *meat*," said Lee hungrily. "We need…"

There was a distant sound of chattering, high in the trees somewhere nearby.

Animal Antics

"Wake up, you lazybones troop! There's food to eat and fur to groom and lots of stuff to do today!"

Morris's ears pricked up at the unmistakable sound of his mother's voice. His night-time adventures had brought him almost all the way home again! Suddenly, he wanted to see his mum more than anything. He had so much to tell her!

Lee had heard the chattering too. His eyes glinted. "Monkeys," he purred. "That's what we need. Branches and branches full of juicy little monkeys."

Animal Antics

Morris almost squeaked aloud with terror. Sammy shot out a paw and covered Morris's mouth to stop him from shouting out.

"I don't like eating branches," said Laz. "The splinters stick in my teeth."

"Shut up, Laz," said Lee. His head was on one side. "I'm listening."

Animal Antics

Be quiet, Mum, Morris prayed. *Be quiet, Marvin!* He knew it was hopeless. His troop never shut up from dawn until dusk, and half the time they yelled through the night as well.

"Gotcha," said Lee, swivelling his head in the direction of the chattering with a satisfied smile on his face. "This way, Laz. They'll be down to feed soon. It'll be as easy as picking fleas off your bottom."

"I don't have fleas."

"You do."

"Do not."

"Do not."

"Uh … do?"

"Ha ha! You said you have fleas!"

"I never!"

Still arguing, the leopards melted away into the mist. Morris pushed Sammy's paw away from his mouth as soon as they had gone.

Animal Antics

"That's my TROOP!" he said urgently. "We have to warn them, Sammy! The leopards are going to eat my mum!"

Sammy heaved off the banana stem and leaves. "OK," he said. "Which way?"

"Easy," said Morris, brushing banana leaves off his shoulders. "Follow the chattering. Just like the leopards are doing!"

Morris gritted his teeth and flung himself at a tree. But he was so flustered that his aim was completely wrong. Instead of landing on a branch, Morris sailed through the leaves and landed on top of Sammy.

"OOF!" said Sammy, rolling over.

"Sorry!" Morris panted, scrabbling back up the tree. "Come ON!"

Animal Antics

Together, the monkey and the sun bear blundered through the jungle. The mist was thickening, and Morris could barely see from tree to tree. Several times he leaped into nothing – and was caught by a pair of big bear paws as he fell. Sammy usually dropped him as soon as he caught him, but it was better than landing head-first on the ground.

Despite the noise Morris and Sammy were making, the leopards were too busy arguing to notice they were being followed.

"You said 'do'. That means you have fleas."

"Did not!"

"Did!"

Morris could still hear his troop screeching and playing in the trees ahead. No one was making the distress call. At this rate, the leopards would have a feast.

Animal Antics

"We're my troop's only hope!" Morris said desperately. "Ow!" he added, crashing into the underside of a heavy vine.

"It never hurts for long," said Sammy, as Morris rubbed his head. "I'll give you a leg up. Whoops… Didn't mean to fling you that far. Are you OK?"

Chapter Eight

Step by step, Morris and Sammy struggled along. Up ahead, Morris caught the leopards' voices again.

"Is this the right way, Lee?"

"Use your ears, Laz!"

"I can't see with my ears, Lee."

"The mist is confusing the leopards," Morris called down softly to Sammy. "But we have to be quieter now we're so close."

He risked jumping a little higher up the trees as Sammy lurched along beneath him. He needed to pass over the leopards' heads if he was to reach his troop first.

The sound of the monkeys chattering and laughing was getting louder. Morris could hear his mum's voice drifting over the top of all the noise.

"…And that starfruit tree over there's just shed its fruit. I heard it fall this morning. Music to my ears."

"Heading down to the ground then, are we?" called another monkey higher up the tree.

"I always say that this time of day's the best time for feeding on the ground. Don't I?" said Morris's mum.

"Yes, you do, boss!" said a different monkey's voice.

"Yeah!" said another.

"What's a ghost's favourite fruit?" piped up Marvin.

"Dunno."

"Boonana. Get it, Mum? *Boonana?* I made that one up just for you."

"You're a terrible creep sometimes," said Morris's mum. "Has anyone seen Morris this morning? He had an awful day yesterday. I hope he's all right."

Morris heard the worry in his mum's voice. He felt ashamed of himself. How could he have thought she'd be glad to see the back of him just because he was clumsy?

"He probably fell out of the tree in the night," said Marvin with a laugh.

"I expect he just spent the night a bit lower down, away from your teasing," Morris's mum replied, sounding cross.

Animal Antics

"So? Are we going down, boss?" boomed Magda.

"Down, down, down!" shouted Marvin.

"In a *minute*," said Morris's mum impatiently. "Let's wait for that lovely mango tree over there to drop its fruit as well. Then we can eat starfruit AND mango, and be back up this tree before you can say 'leopard'."

Morris only had a few moments left to stop the monkeys from heading to their doom! He scanned the misty treetops in search of his family – and stopped in dismay.

They were sitting at the very top of Morris's least favourite tree. It was bendy and whip-thin. It lurched and flung itself about like a crazed snake whenever Morris went near it.

Morris swallowed. Could he shout out and warn them? His troop was making so much noise, they probably wouldn't hear him.

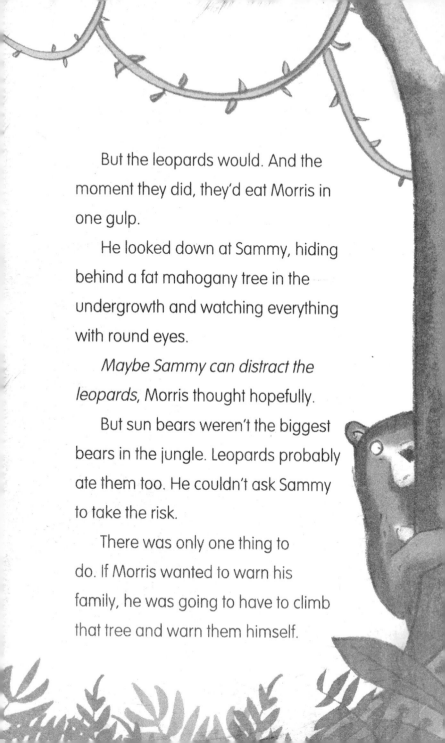

But the leopards would. And the moment they did, they'd eat Morris in one gulp.

He looked down at Sammy, hiding behind a fat mahogany tree in the undergrowth and watching everything with round eyes.

Maybe Sammy can distract the leopards, Morris thought hopefully.

But sun bears weren't the biggest bears in the jungle. Leopards probably ate them too. He couldn't ask Sammy to take the risk.

There was only one thing to do. If Morris wanted to warn his family, he was going to have to climb that tree and warn them himself.

The hairs on the back of his neck stood up in fright as he heard the leopards talking beneath him. He was much closer to them than he'd realized. If he dangled his tail, he could tickle the one called Laz on the nose.

Animal Antics

"There must be thirty monkeys up that tree, Laz. We'll split them down the middle: twenty for me and ten for you."

"That ain't right, Lee."

"OK. Twenty-five for me and five for you."

"That's better!" Laz gave a nasty snigger. "I'll just sharpen my claws. You need really sharp ones for splitting monkeys down the middle."

"We're not *actually* splitting them down the middle, Laz. I like my monkeys whole, thanks very much."

"You said we was! I wanna split them down the middle!"

Morris watched and waited. Surely someone in the troop would hear the leopards and give the warning? But no one was listening. Excited voices drifted down through the mist.

Animal Antics

"Bet you those mangoes fall off before I count to five. One, two…"

"Race you!"

"Race you first!"

It was now or never. Morris looked across to his least favourite tree. The gap was wider than he would have liked, and the morning mist was making it hard to see. If he got it wrong, he'd land right on top of the leopards. But it was a risk he had to take.

He shut his eyes tightly and jumped.

Chapter Nine

By some miracle, Morris landed just right. Below him, Lee's voice rang out through the mist.

"Something moved above us. Did you hear it, Laz?"

"Juicy little monkeys, I expect, Lee. Can we pounce yet? Can we?"

"I told you, we can't get them till they're on the ground. That tree won't hold our weight."

Animal Antics

Morris scrambled up to the next branch, his heart racing with fear.

"You again?" said the spotty bug.

"I thought we'd seen the last of you," said the stripey one.

"Why have you come back?" said the plain one.

"Get out of my way!" Morris hissed. He stamped hard on the branch. The bugs dropped away with a soft *plop-plop-plop*. Morris climbed on up, staying as close to the tree's thin trunk as he could. Any minute now, he expected to feel the leopards' hot breath on his tail.

Back at the top of the tree, the troop were chanting at the mango tree in loud monkey voices. "Drop, drop, drop your fruit… DROP, DROP, DROP YOUR FRUIT…"

Morris was way above the leopards now. "Stop!" he shouted up the tree. "Don't move!"

He heard his mum's voice drifting over the top of the chanting. "I just heard Morris. Did you hear Morris, Marvin?"

"Was he saying 'ouch'?"

"No, he— Ooh! There go the mangoes!"

There was a swish of mangoes falling from high above. They hurtled past Morris and hit the ground with a squish, their warm fruity smell wafting back up through the mist. The troop hollered with delight.

"Don't go down there!" shouted Morris, who was now halfway up the tree and climbing as fast as he dared. "Listen to me, please listen to me!"

"Well well, look who it is. Bit high for you up here, isn't it, little brother?" Marvin said slyly, appearing suddenly beside Morris. "Race you to the mangoes, if you're monkey enough!"

"Marvin!" howled Morris, trying to turn round on the branch and chase after his brother. The tree wobbled horribly. "Don't— Aaaahhhh!"

He was falling. Branches whipped at his legs. Twigs scraped through his fur. Head over heels he went, bump, bump, bump down the trunk…

Animal Antics

"OOF!"

…Smack bang into Sammy on the ground.

Before Morris could thank the sun bear for saving him – again – Sammy pushed Morris down.

"Shhh!" Sammy whispered.

The two leopards were crouched beneath a tangle of vines a few metres away, gazing up the tall thin tree with hungry eyes. They were concentrating so hard that they hadn't seen Sammy or noticed Morris's top-speed descent.

"Mangoes, mangoes, for my tea!" sang Marvin, leading the way down the tree. "Mangoes, mangoes, so yum-my! Mangoes, mangoes, all for ME!"

"I'll distract the leopards," said Sammy suddenly, standing up. "You stop your troop."

He blundered over to the nearby fallen fruit.

"Yum," he said loudly. "Mangoes. My favourite."

The leopards stared round at Sammy in surprise, just as Marvin neared the ground.

"GET BACK UP THE TREE, MARVIN!" Morris shouted.

Animal Antics

Marvin puffed out his chest. "Don't talk to me like that, you clumsy little—"

But the leopards had heard. "I want a MONKEY!" roared Lee, spinning away from Sammy.

"I want TWO!" growled Laz.

Everything happened at once. Marvin shrieked with terror and sprang back up into the whippy branches overhead, just avoiding Laz's shining claws. As Lee hurled himself towards Morris, Morris grabbed Marvin's tail and zoomed up the tree after his brother. The rest of the troop, who were almost at the bottom of the tree, stopped, screamed and raced to the top again. And Sammy lurched towards Laz, skidded in the pile of starfruit, slipped in the mangoes, trod on Lee's tail – and fell against the monkeys' tree with a bone-shaking THUMP.

Chapter Ten

"Whoops!" cried Sammy, as the tree trunk started to bend backwards.

"Let's get out of here!" shouted Laz. "That bear nearly squashed me!"

"Don't leave me behind!" howled Lee. "He'll tread on my tail again!"

The leopards scarpered.

Monkeys were hanging on to the tree for

dear life all around Morris. Even Marvin was too busy wrapping his long arms round the trunk to complain about the tight grip Morris still had on his tail. Magda was hanging upside down, a baby monkey in each arm. "Hang in there!" she bellowed. "That's the ticket!"

Groaning as it went, the tree bent further and further backwards until Sammy was almost lying flat on his back and staring up at the canopy roof. Then…

TWANNNGGG.

The whole tree pinged up again like a catapult. Sammy was hurled across the jungle floor, landing in a prickly-looking bush. As for the monkeys, it was impossible to hold on now. Morris's entire troop zoomed from the branches like a flock of furry brown birds, arms and legs and tails waving helplessly.

Animal Antics

"Whaaa!"

"Help!"

"Whee!"

Magda started booming instructions, still with a baby monkey clamped in each paw. "Stretch out your arms, if you can! Use your tails to balance yourselves!"

Morris cartwheeled through the misty air. It was quite nice really. He didn't know which way was up and which was down. He opened his eyes dreamily. Then he wished he hadn't. He was about to slam into a kapok tree face first.

"Take my paw, Morris!" Marvin shouted, dangling towards him from one of the tree's long branches.

Morris grasped Marvin's paw and came to an abrupt stop. He swung in the air like a hairy pendulum for a few moments.

"Thanks," he panted. He looked cautiously up at his brother. "I suppose you're going to drop me now because it's funny?"

"You saved my life, so I saved your head," said Marvin. He pulled Morris up beside him. "That means we're quits. Right?"

Morris sat on the branch beside his big brother, catching his breath. The troop had all landed safely. Most of them were already down on the jungle floor looking for what was left of the mangoes. Sammy was pulling thorns out of his bottom and chatting to Magda.

We did it! Morris thought in wonder. *Sammy and I saved them from the leopards!*

He swelled with happiness, pride and – perhaps for the first time in his life – a feeling of confidence.

What a difference one little night-time adventure can make, he thought.

Animal Antics

Morris's mother jumped on to the branch beside Morris. She gave him a warm hug. "We were worried about you, Morris," she said. "It's good to see you safe and sound."

"Thanks to me," Marvin said quickly. "I caught him and saved him. Don't forget that."

Morris decided not to point out that he'd saved Marvin from the leopards first. He gave a dramatic gasp instead. "Look, Marvin!" he said. "The leopards are back!"

As Marvin swivelled his head in alarm, Morris shoved him hard in the back. Marvin toppled off the branch and fell into the same prickly bush Sammy had just climbed out of.

"Ouch!" Marvin howled.

"I'm sorry, what was that, Marvin?" said Morris cheerfully, cupping his paw behind his ear.

"I said, OUCH!"

"What a cheek," sniffed the spotty bug.

He was watching Morris playing a game with some of the other monkeys, as the troop prepared to go to bed. Morris was dangling upside down on a branch, but he soon fell off, landing with a bump on his head. Laughing, he climbed back up on to the branch again.

"Reckons he's a monkey again, does he?" said the stripey one. "Who does he think he's fooling?"

"Not me, that's for sure," said the plain one.

"Excuse me?" said a fourth voice.

The bugs' beetly little eyes widened.

"Hmm," said Pan, swallowing them down in one go. "Bugs taste almost as nice as ants."

And a bit more...

"…So you was going to give me five monkeys, was it, Lee?"

"Yes, Laz."

"But we didn't get no monkeys at all, right, Lee?"

"That's right, Laz."

"So, you owes me… You owes me…"

"One monkey, Laz."

"Yeah. One monkey. Yeah."

THE
END

Totally True

Pangolins shut their nostrils when feeding to stop the ants running up their noses.

Some monkeys burp at their friends for fun.

Shake any rainforest tree and up to 1,500 different types of insect may fall out.

Only 6% of the land on Earth is covered by rainforest, but half of all the world's species live there.

A full-grown rainforest tree's branches can stretch out as wide as a football pitch.

Sun bears are pigeon-toed.

Coming soon:

Animal Antics

The Scaredy Bear